Changes, Changes
Cambios, cambios

Changes, Changes
Cambios, cambios

PAT HUTCHINS

TeachingStrategies® · Bethesda, MD

ISBN 978-1-60617-225-4

CPSIA tracking label information:
RR Donnelley, Shenzhen, China
Date of Production: August 2016
Cohort: Batch 5
Printed and bound in China

9	16
Printing	Year Printed

THE LIBRARY OF CONGRESS HAS CATALOGED THE SIMON & SCHUSTER EDITION AS FOLLOWS:

Hutchins, Pat, date.
   Changes, Changes

Summary: Two wooden dolls rearrange wooden building blocks to form various objects.
   [1. Toys—Fiction. 2. Stories without words]
I. Title
[PZ7.H96165Ch 1987] [E] 86-22331

For Elsie and Bob Bruce

Para Elsie y Bob Bruce